November 22, 2006

To Lindsey from
Grandma Chrissy

My Dog Wears Shoes and Her Name Is
MAGGIE MAE

Written by
Laurie Fitzgerald

Illustrations by
Dana Howe

BOOK PUBLISHERS NETWORK

Published by

Book Publishers Network

P. O. Box 2256

Bothell, WA 98041

425 483-3040

ISBN 1-887542-30-2

LCCN: 2005934751

Printed in China

10 9 8 7 6 5 4 3 2

Book Design: Laura Zugzda

Dedication

This book is dedicated to my mother, "Bebe," who gave me the inspiration to pursue this book. To my family and friends who gave me the encouragment to finish the book. To my dear friend Dana, who through her great talent, made all my dreams come true.

And finally, to my incredible husband Jim who put it all together and gave me the faith. I thank you all.

And oh, I almost forgot my dear Maggie Mae, who without her there would be no story.

Laurie

My dog wears shoes.
Her name is "Maggie Mae."
She wears them to go out.
She wears them to play.

She wears her red shoes when she is going to the mall.

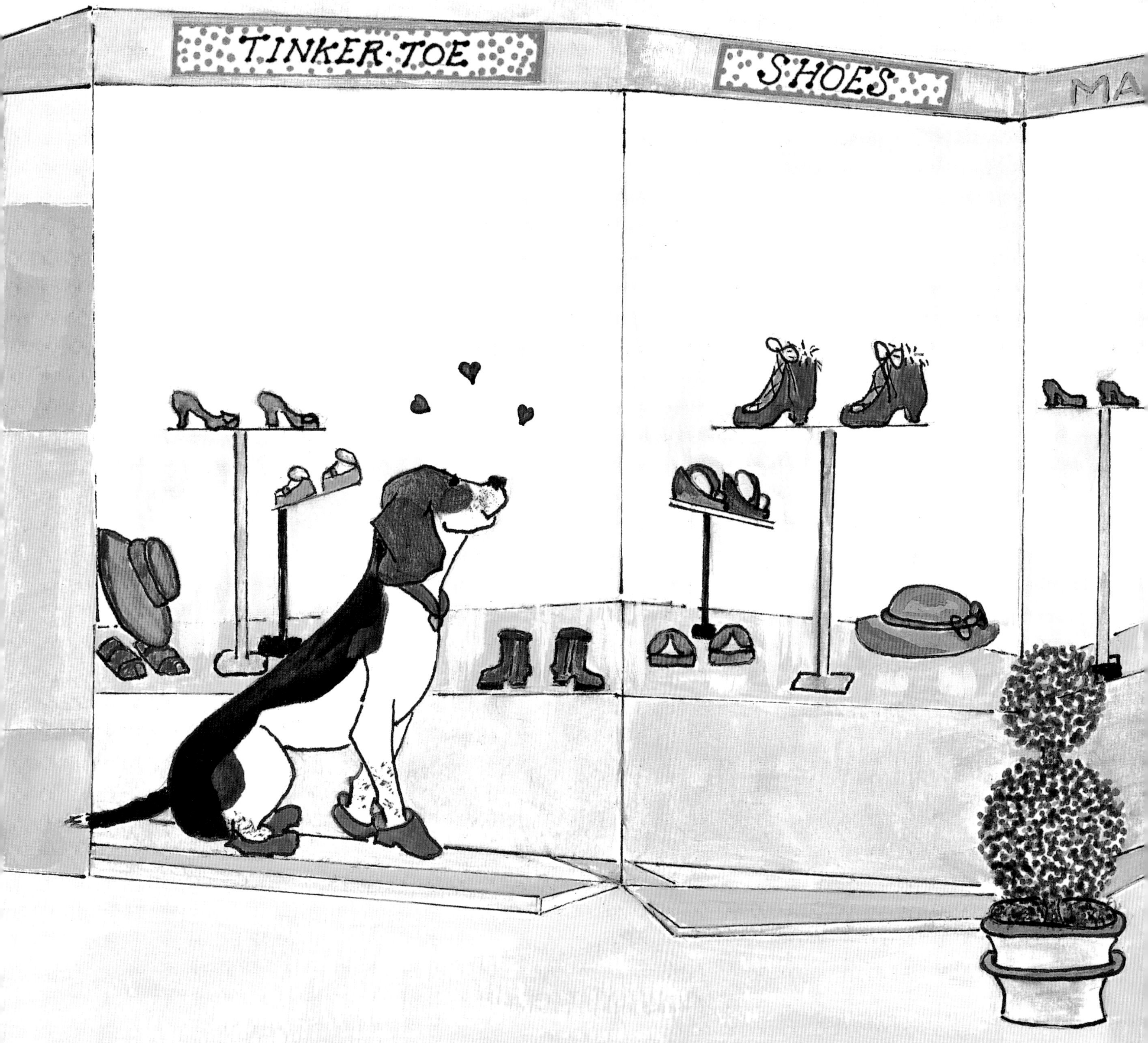
TINKER·TOE
SHOES

She wears her blue shoes
when she is playing ball.

She wears her green shoes
to take a walk in the park.

She wears her pink shoes
when she is dancing in the dark.

You see, my dog Maggie Mae,
she loves to wear shoes.

She wears her lavender shoes
when she is out picking roses.

She wears her orange shoes
when she is doing doggie poses.

She wears her yellow shoes
when she is walking in the rain.

She wears her *black patent shoes*
when she is going on a plane.

You see, my dog Maggie Mae, she loves to wear shoes.

She wears her magenta slippers when she is lounging on the couch and sometimes catches a glimpse of a mouse.

She wears her white tennis shoes to do
her daily run, and this is by far,
to her, the most fun.

Her purple shoes are a must,
even though she is only riding
on a bus.

Her bath time is such a treat, because it so delights her feet. She grabs her golden flippers and quietly takes off her afternoon slippers.

At the end of the day, all worn out
from work and play, Maggie Mae
puts her shoes away. In a special little
place right under the bed, she has
her shoes facing straight ahead.

You see, my dog Maggie Mae,
she loves to wear shoes. So, the next time
you see her, you'll be in for a treat. Who knows
what she will have on her soft and tender feet?

The Maggie Mae Foundation

Wherever you live, there are children of all ages who are in desperate need of adequate shoes for school and play. A portion of the sales of this book will go towards fulfilling that need. That is the purpose of "The Maggie Mae Foundation."

If you would like to personally donate additional funds for this cause, please send your tax-deductible donation to:

Shoes That Fit
1420 N. Claremont Blvd., Suite 107-B
Claremont, CA 91711
888-715-4333

Or make a donation online at
www.shoesthatfit.org

When making a donation, please note "Maggie Mae Foundation" in the memo line.

The mission of Shoes That Fit is to help build the self-esteem of school children in need by providing them with new shoes and clothes.

Thank you,
Maggie Mae